Behold
the
Trees

Behold the Trees

BY SUE ALEXANDER

ILLUSTRATED BY LEONID GORE

ARTHUR A. LEVINE BOOKS
AN IMPRINT OF SCHOLASTIC PRESS

LIBRARY OF CONGRESS CATALOGING-IN-PUBLICATION DATA

Alexander, Sue.
Behold the trees / by Sue Alexander; illustrated by Leonid Gore.   p.   cm.
Summary: A land once protected by all sorts of wonderful trees is reduced over time
by war and environmental neglect to desert, until new inhabitants plant trees and
slowly make Israel bloom again.

ISBN 0-590-76211-7

[1. Trees—Fiction. 2. Israel—Fiction.] I. Gore, Leonid, ill. II. Title.
PZ7.A3784Bg   2000 [Fic]—dc21   99-25114

Text type was set in 14-point Garamond 3 and AGaramond Small Caps.
The display type was hand-lettered by John Stevens.
The illustrations were done in acrylic paint and colored pencils on paper.
Book design by Marijka Kostiw

10 9 8 7 6 5 4 3 2 1   01 02 03 04 05

Printed in Singapore on acid-free paper   46
First edition, March 2001

GRATEFUL ACKNOWLEDGMENT MUST GO

TO THE JEWISH NATIONAL FUND AND ITS

MILLIONS OF CONTRIBUTORS ALL OVER

THE WORLD, WITHOUT WHOM THERE

WOULD HAVE BEEN NO STORY TO TELL.

SPECIAL THANKS TO GAIL VIDA GOLOD

IN ISRAEL AND MAXINE DEARBORN

IN THE UNITED STATES FOR THEIR

INVALUABLE HELP WITH MY RESEARCH.

THIS BOOK IS DEDICATED

WITH LOVE TO MY FOREVER FRIEND,

MAXINE DEARBORN

— S. A.

TO MY PARENTS

— L. G.

Trees. Leaves, twigs, branches, bark-covered

trunks, roots going down into dark, damp soil.

Shields for the earth against the searing sun

and drying winds.

This is the story of one land and its trees.

It begins a long, long, very long time ago...

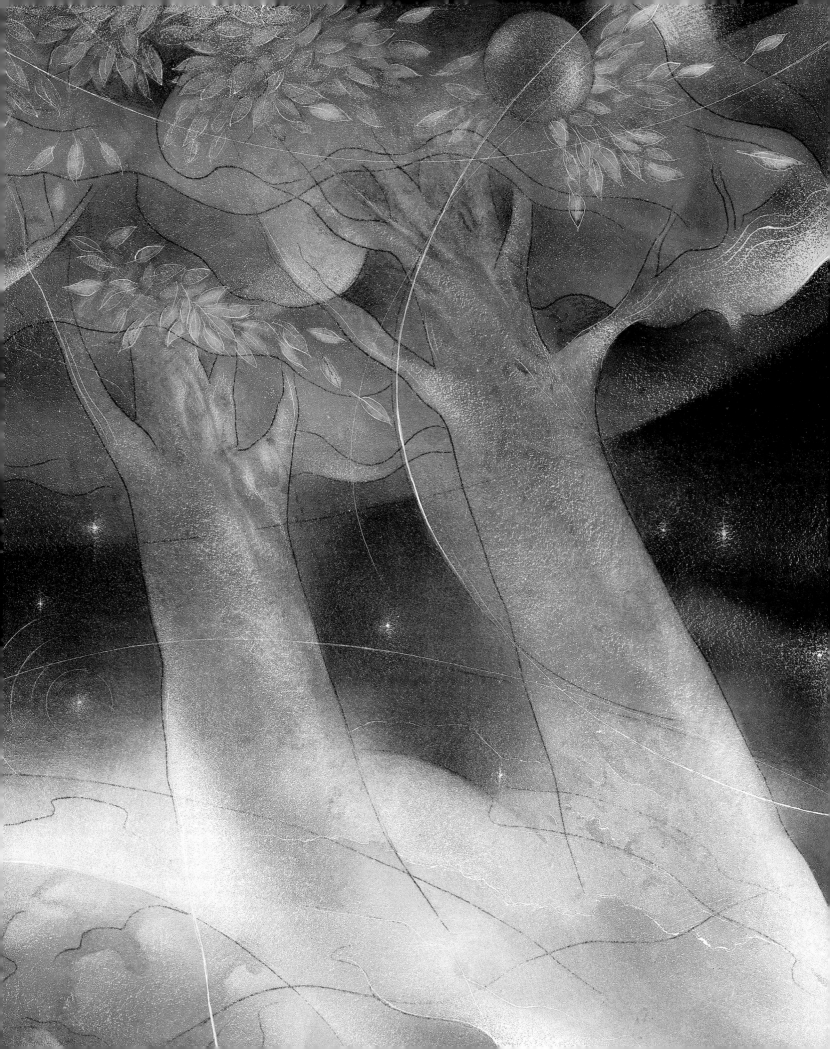

Oak and almond, fig and olive, terebinth and palm, acacia and pomegranate, willow and tamarisk. They grew wild when the land was called Canaan. They grew at the edge of the Great Sea, in the valleys and on the hillsides, along the shore of the Sea of Chinnereth, and on the oases of the wilderness.

Living, life-giving trees.

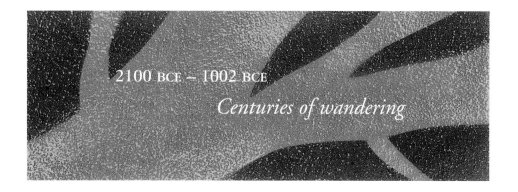

They grew in stands and groves and great forests. They held back the sea, cooled the air, and protected the earth for the people and animals who lived there.

Shepherds rested in their shade and travelers ate their fruits. Doves nested in their branches and gazelles ate their tender green leaves.

So it was, for hundreds and hundreds of years, through the centuries of wandering — the time of Abraham, Isaac and Jacob, and the Israelites who came after them.

Then, in the years of the kings — Saul, David, and Solomon — many shepherds ceased roaming the land. Some became farmers. Others became craftsmen. New towns and cities came into being.

And the cutting down of the trees began.

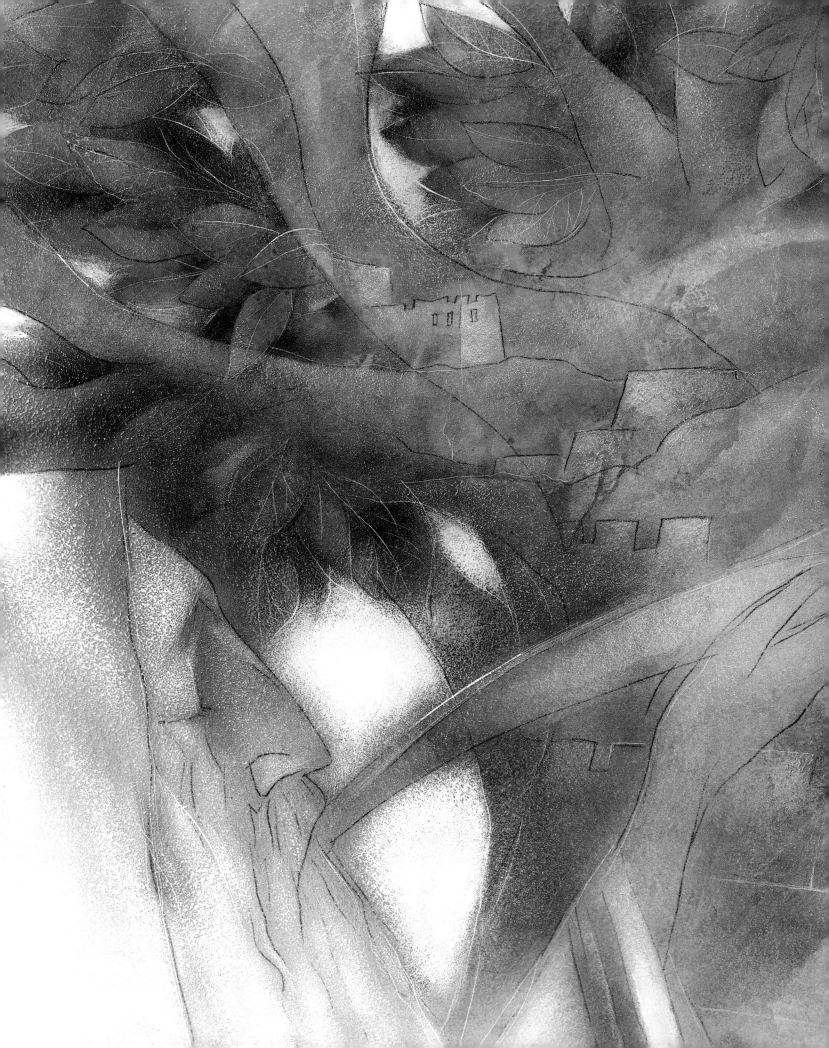

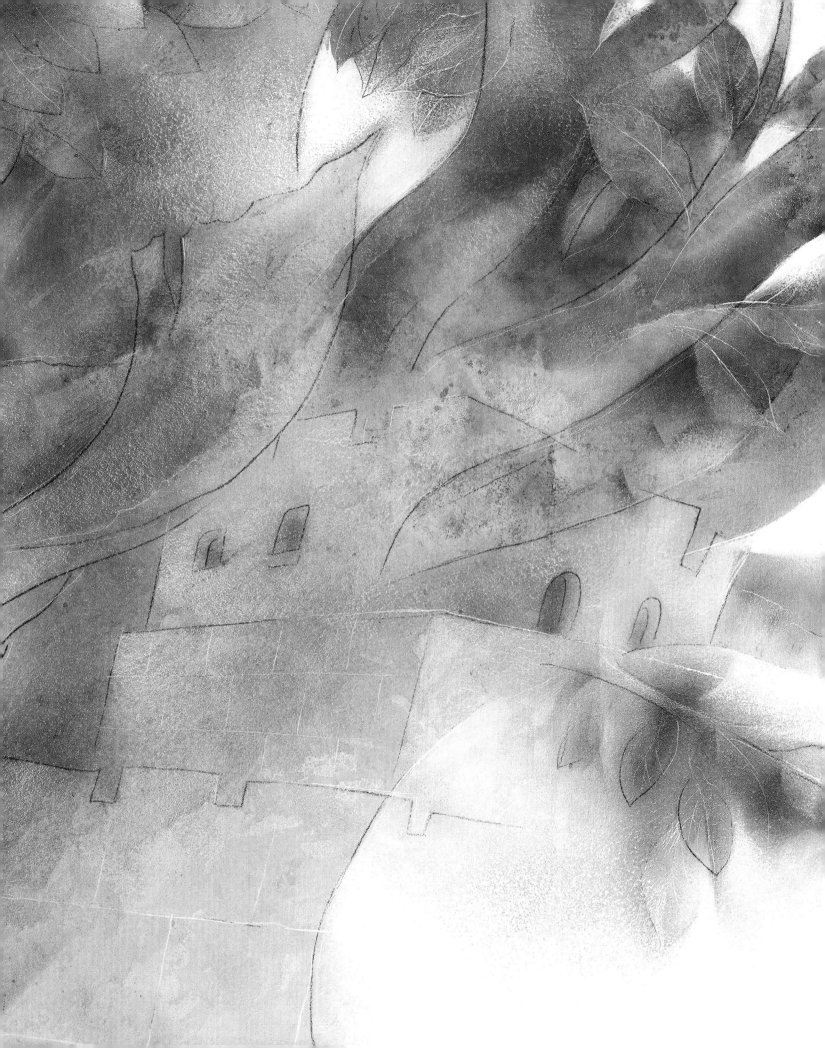

Fields were cleared, plowed, and planted. Wooden doors were made for homes and shops in the towns and cities. Stables and sheds were built. Fires sent twists of smoke into the air as people cooked and warmed themselves when the cold winds blew.

And no new trees were planted to take the place of those that were cut down.

But trees still grew on the hillsides, in the valleys, along the shores of the seas, and on the oases of the wilderness.

Living, life-giving trees.

So it was, through a siege of wars that lasted more than six hundred years. One after another, the armies of Assyria, Babylonia, Persia, Greece, and Rome swept through the land, destroying what had been built. The Romans called the land Palestine and, like each of the armies before them, cut down trees to build fortresses and palaces, shrines to their gods, cities and towns.

And no new trees were planted.

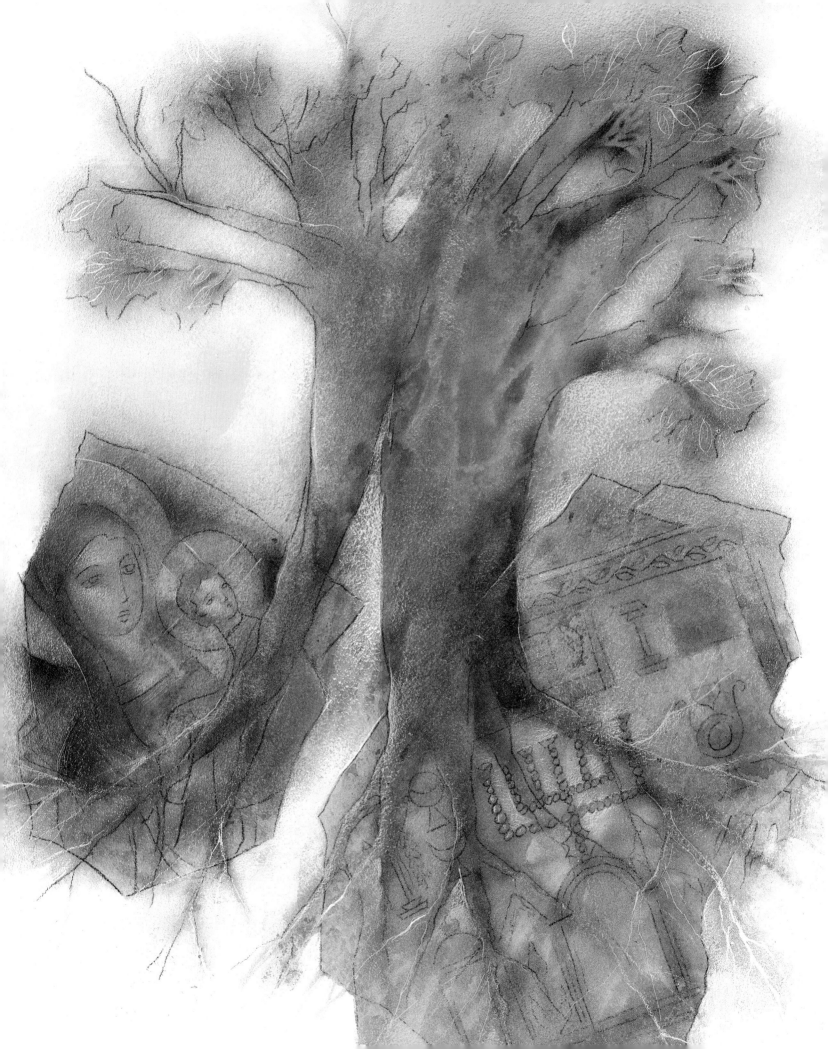

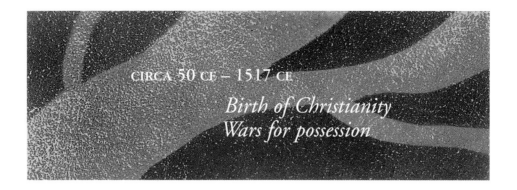

But trees still grew in stands and groves and great forests. They still held back the sea, cooled the air, and protected the earth for the people and animals who lived there.

So it was, through the days of Jesus, James and John, Peter and Paul, and the Christians who came after them.

In the hundreds of years that followed, more wars were fought for possession of the land, and more and more trees were lost. Soldiers cut down trees to build catapults and wheeled shooting towers, and burned whole forests so their enemies would have no place to hide. With fire and swords they destroyed the trees that grew along the shore of the sea so no invader's ships could come upon them unseen.

And no new trees were planted.

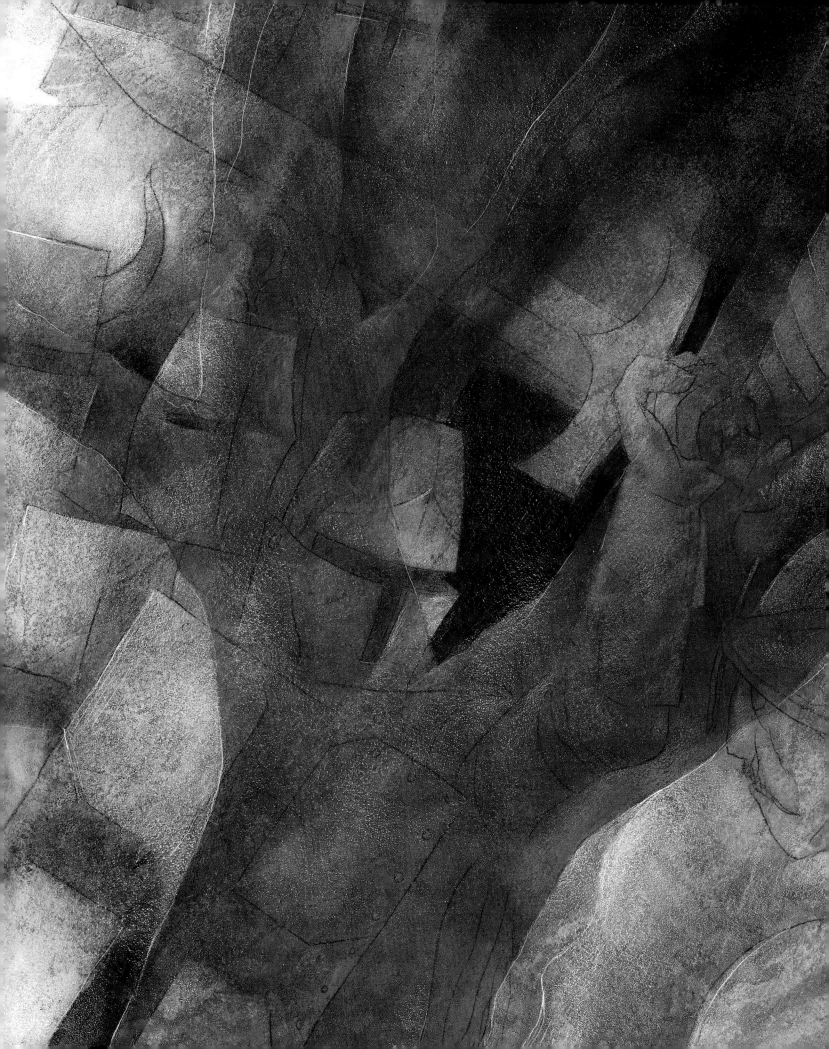

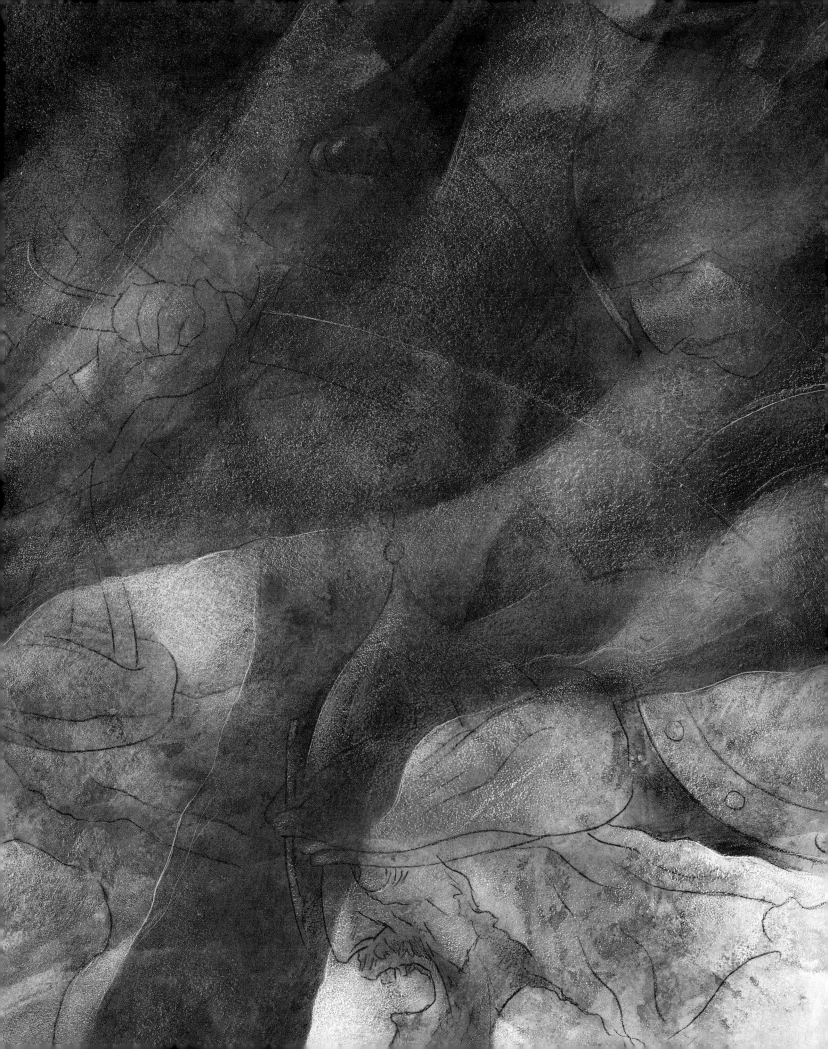

Through the years, many mosques and churches had been built and people began to come from around the world to visit what had come to be called the Holy Land. The Turks, who now ruled the land, ordered trees to be cut down to build roads and bridges, tracks for trains, and places for travelers to stay.

Over time, the Turks began to fight among themselves and with other nations. And the land was ignored. Farms were abandoned and cities and towns were deserted. Black goats roamed freely eating all the plants and chewing up trees by their roots.

1882 CE – 1914 CE
Settlers plant first groves
World War 1 begins

Then, a little more than a hundred years ago, a group of

Jewish settlers came to the land. They tried to plow and plant, but

little would grow. So they began to plant trees. First they planted

a small grove of olive trees, and then one of cypress and pine.

But again, war spread throughout the land. Most of the trees

in the last of the forests were split into ties for railroad tracks. The

rest became fuel for the trains.

Few trees remained.

Oak and almond, fig and olive, terebinth and palm, acacia and pomegranate, willow and tamarisk. They no longer grew in the valleys, on the hillsides, or along the shores of the seas and on the oases of the wilderness. There were few wild stands or groves and no more great forests. There were not enough trees left to hold back the sea, cool the air, or protect the earth.

And the land became salt marsh and sand.

Without trees to sustain them, the animals and birds disappeared. Gazelles and antelope no longer roamed the hillsides or lingered in the valleys. No owls or doves remained to soar through the air or trill their songs.

After the war was over, more people came to settle on the land. They lived in abandoned buildings and tents.

And they planted trees.

In homes and shops all over the world, Jewish people had been putting pence and pounds, centimes and francs, pfennigs and marks, centavos and pesos, guilders, rands, florins, dimes and dollars into small blue banks to buy trees for the land. They celebrated happy events in their lives and commemorated sad ones by giving money to plant trees.

1939 CE – 1945 CE
World War II

Then, during another great war less than half a century later, many

Jewish people sought shelter in the arid land. After the war, they

built their own villages, towns, and cities.

And they planted trees.

Old people, middle-aged people, and young people dug the

earth and, month after month, year after year, planted — one by one

— hundreds and thousands and millions of trees.

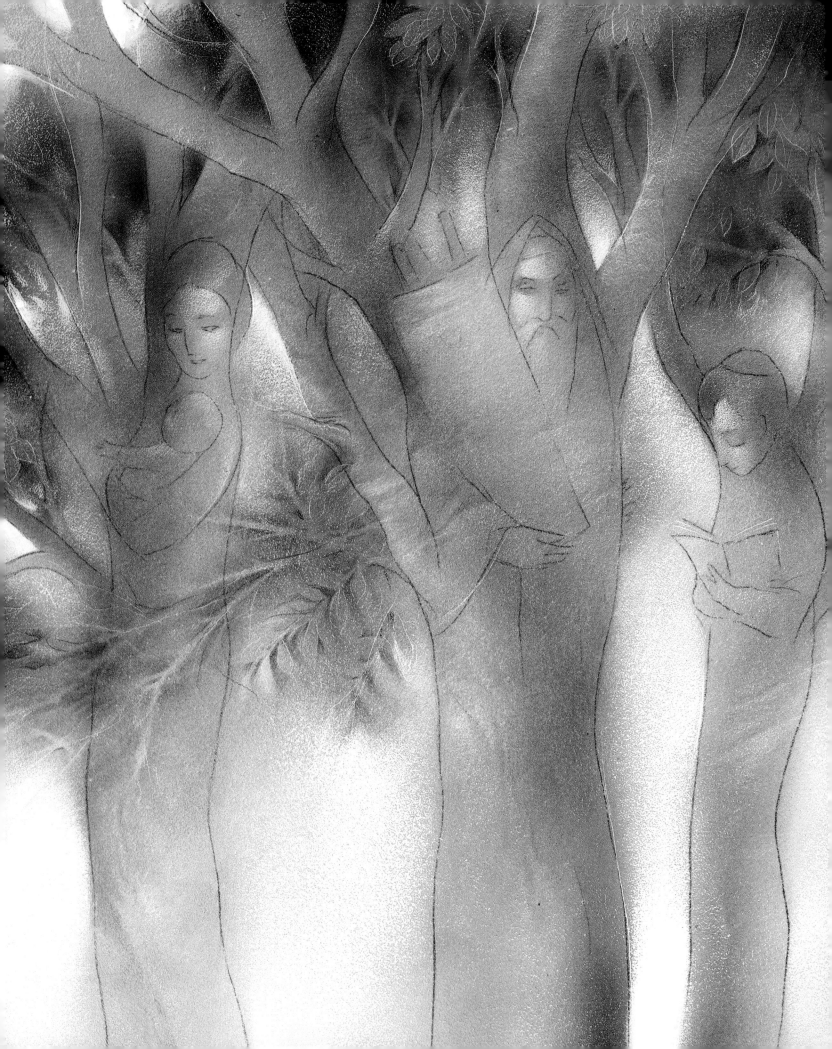

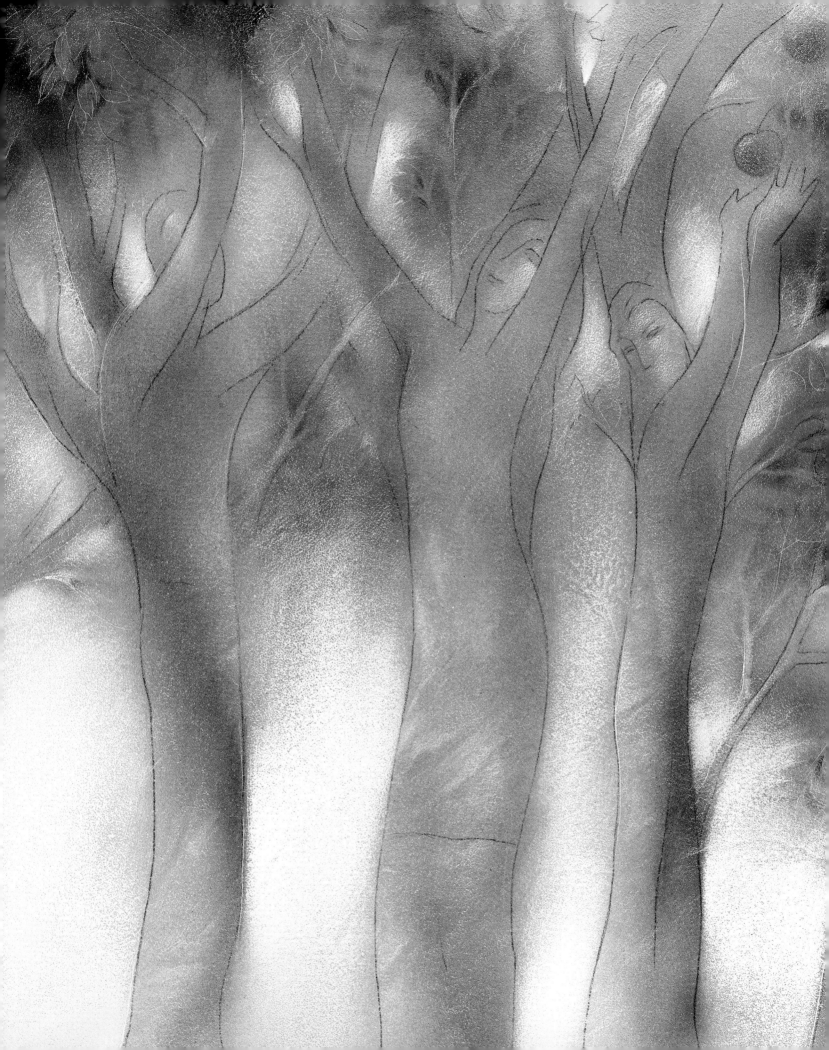

Cypress and pine, eucalyptus and acacia, orange and olive, lemon and pecan, oak and palm. They all grow now in the land called Israel. They grow at the edge of the Mediterranean Sea, in the valleys and on the hillsides, along the shore of the Sea of Galilee and in the wilderness. They grow in stands and groves and great forests. They hold back the sea, cool the air, and protect the earth for the people and animals who live there.

Behold
the
Trees

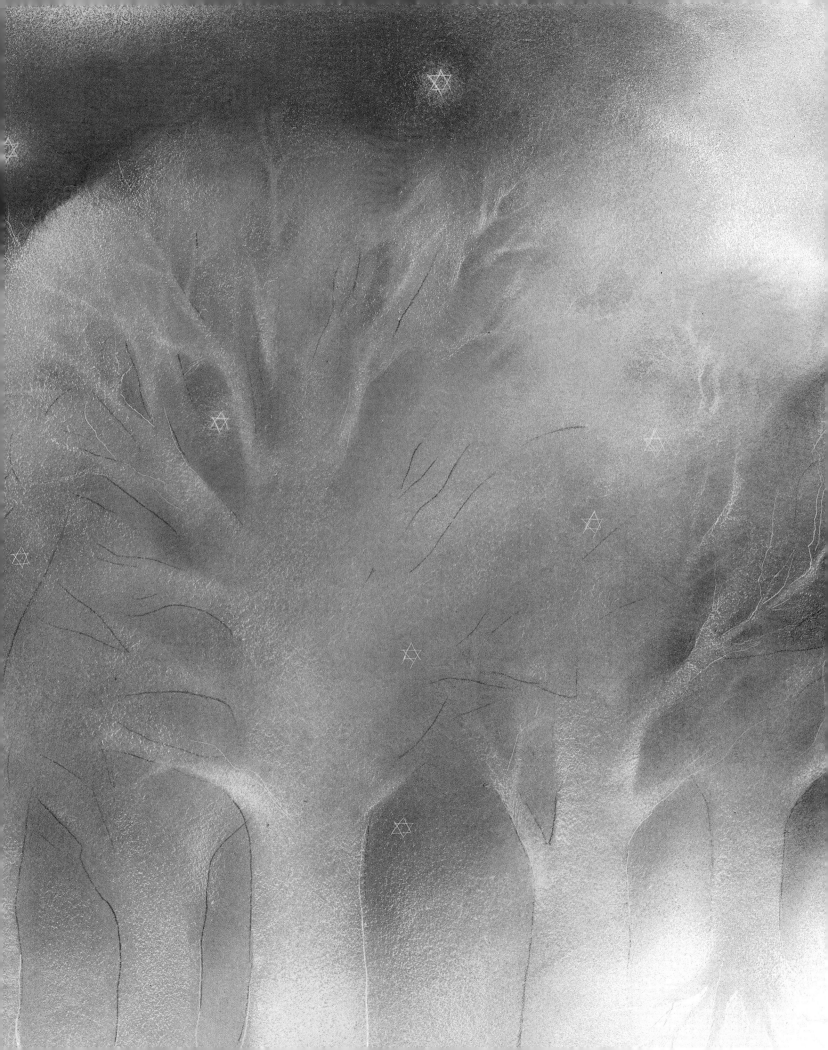

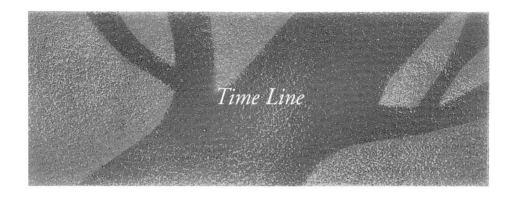

Time Line

AS WRITTEN RECORDS DO NOT EXIST FOR MUCH OF EARLY HISTORY, THE TIME FRAMES

GIVEN WERE DETERMINED BY A CONSENSUS OF THE MAJORITY OF SOURCES IN MY RESEARCH

AND ARE INTENDED ONLY TO PROVIDE A GENERAL SENSE OF THE TIME PERIODS INVOLVED.

5000 BCE — 2100 BCE	Canaan
2100 BCE — 1002 BCE	Centuries of wandering
1002 BCE — 608 BCE	Years of the kings (SAUL – ZEDEKIAH)
721 BCE — 63 BCE	Siege of wars (ASSYRIA, BABYLONIA, PERSIA, GREECE, ROME)
63 BCE — 300 CE	Roman rule; land called Palestine
300 CE — 600 CE	Byzantine Empire rule
CIRCA 33 CE	Jesus proclaimed leader
CIRCA 50 CE — 57 CE	Birth of Christianity
600s CE — 1517 CE	Wars for possession (MOSLEMS, CRUSADERS, MAMALUKES, OTTOMAN TURKS)
1517 CE — 1918 CE	Turkish rule
1882 CE	Turks begin to sell parcels of land First Jewish settlers plant first two groves of trees
1884 CE — 1897 CE	Beginning of collection of money by Jews in Europe for land and trees in Palestine
1914 CE — 1918 CE	World War I (LAST FORESTS CUT DOWN)
1918 CE — 1948 CE	British rule More Jewish settlers come, buy land, and plant trees
1939 CE — 1945 CE	World War II Fleeing the war, Jewish people come to Palestine, buy more land, and begin to plant more trees
1948 CE	Independent State of Israel Planting of trees begins in full force

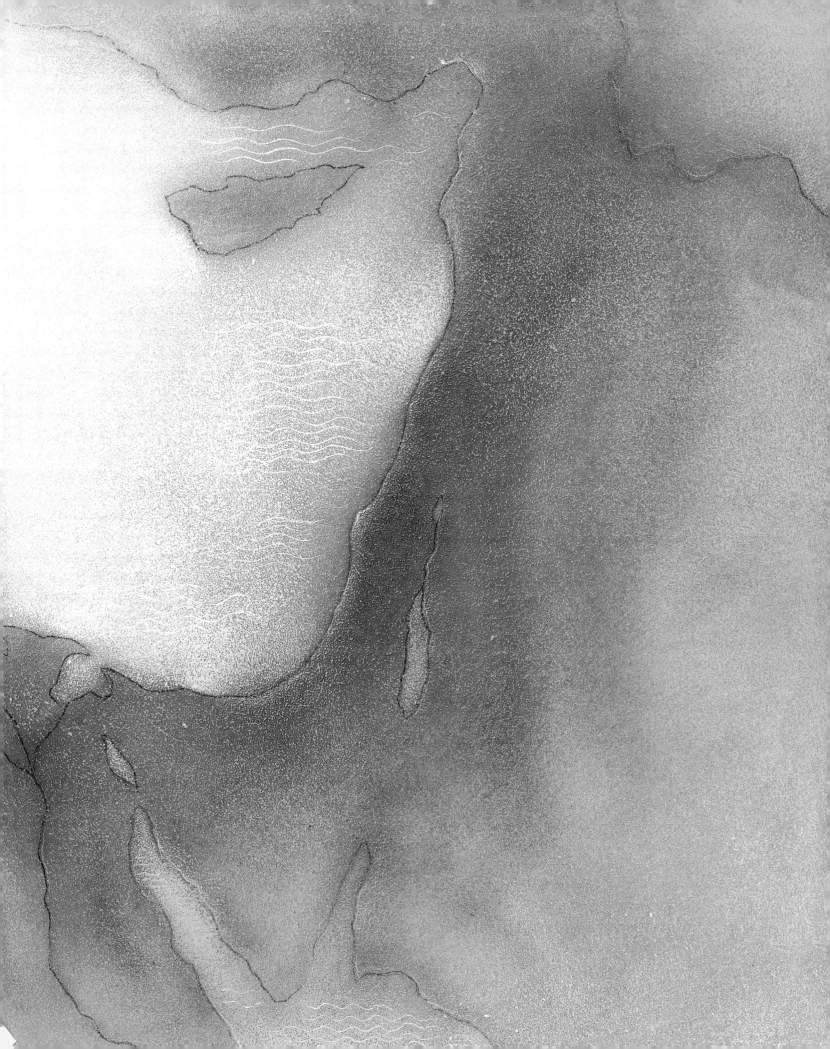

The tree-planting holiday in Israel is called Tu B'Shevat, named for the day on which it is celebrated—the fifteenth day of the month of Shevat, which falls sometime in January or February. Tu B'Shevat evolved from an ancient holiday, Rosh Hashanah L'eilanot (New Year of the Trees), which was also held in the month of Shevat and included the custom of Hamishah Asar, the planting of a tree sapling for each child born during that year.

The importance of trees to human life is acknowledged in many cultures and countries throughout the world by festivals, holidays, or customs involving the planting of trees. In the United States and Canada, the tree-planting holiday is called Arbor Day and is celebrated in almost every state and province.